VANISHING VALENTINES

By Robin Wasserman
Illustrated by Duendes del Sur

Hello Reader — Level 1

ISBN 0-439-31846-7

12 11 10 6/0

Designed by Maria Stasavage
Printed in the U.S.A.
First Scholastic printing, January 2002

SCHOLASTIC INC.
New York Toronto London Auckland Sydney
Mexico City New Delhi Hong Kong Buenos Aires

 and his friends were sad.

It was Valentine's Day.

But no one had sent them a

 or  .

They had no  at all!

They went to see the  .

“Where is our  ?” asked  .

The  was sad, too.

“The  is missing,” he said.

MAIL

“Zoinks!” said . “Maybe a  ran away with our valentines!”

“Ra !” cried .

He hid behind a .

"Come out, ," said .

"We need to find the ."

shook his head. The

shook, too.

"What about your valentine?"

asked . "Maybe someone

sent you some and they

are missing!"

"Ro-kay!" said . He came

out from behind the .

The  took them to Miss Feldman's .

"This is the last place I saw my  of ," he said. "I went to Miss Feldman's . I left the  in my , and I left my   open."

MAIL

"When I came back, my 

of was gone!" said the

.

"Jinkies!" said . She found

a clue.

 found a piece of  in

the .

 found a clue, too. He ate it.

 found more clues.

He ate them, too.

 followed the clues across

the .

He followed them under a .

MAIL

 followed the clues all the

way to the !

 found a pile of 

.

He also found a pile of .

Would a  eat ?

No, but a  would!

MAIL

Now everyone was happy.

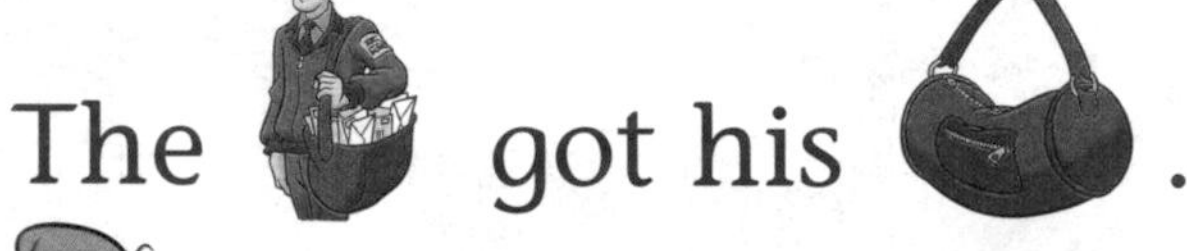

The  got his .

 got a   from his cousin Maggie.

 and  got a 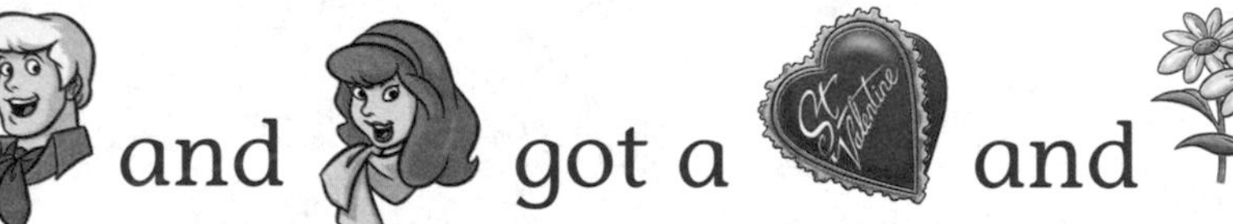 and  from their friend Sally.

 got a stuffed  from her aunt Susan.

But wait! was not happy.

Where was 's valentine gift?

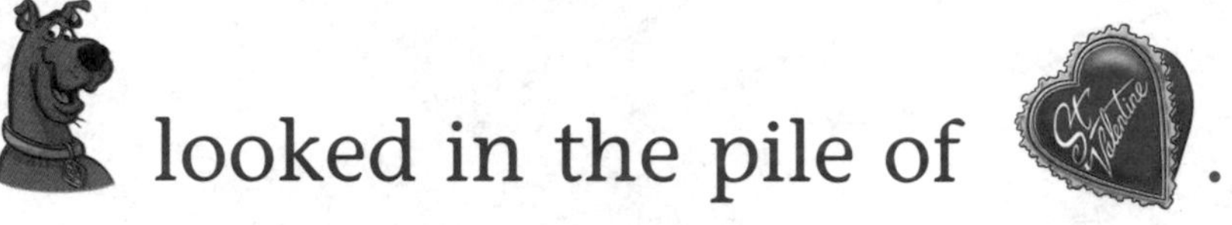

looked in the pile of .

No valentine.

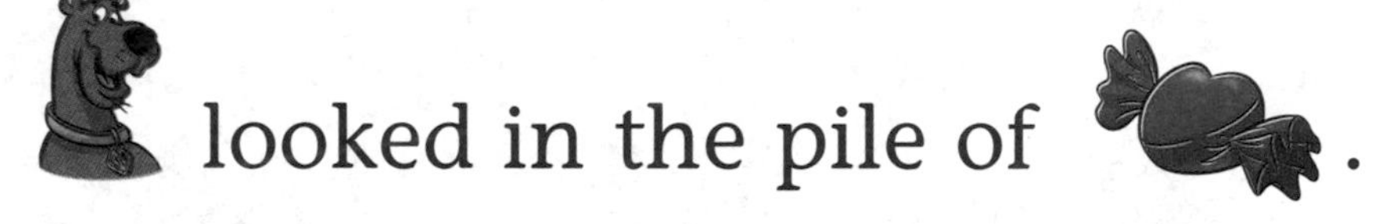

looked in the pile of .

No valentine.

Then [Scooby-Doo] looked behind him.

And he found his valentine!

Someone had sent him a box of [Scooby Snacks]. Now he felt happy.

Happy Valentine's Day, [Scooby-Doo]!

SCOOBY
SNACKS

Did you spot all the picture clues in this Scooby-Doo mystery?

Each picture clue is on a flash card. Ask a grown-up to cut out the flash cards. Then try reading the words on the back of the cards. The pictures will be your clue.

Reading is fun with Scooby-Doo!

St Valentine

card

Scooby

mail

flowers

Fred

mailman

SCOOBY
SNACKS

ghost

Shaggy

Velma

bush

house

Scooby Snacks

MAIL

door

bag

window

truck

grass

candy

fence

street

heart

dog

bear

Daphne